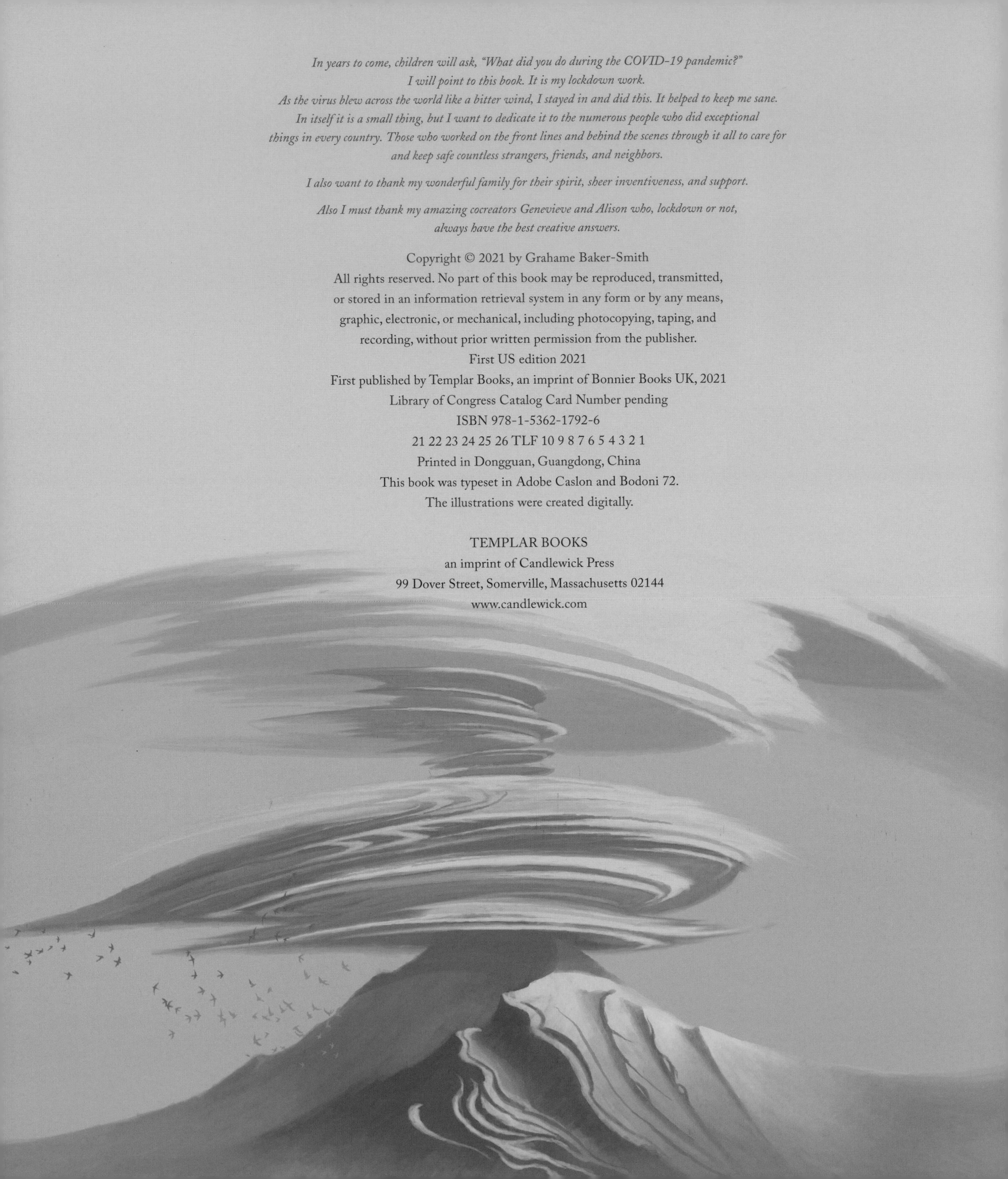

In years to come, children will ask, "What did you do during the COVID-19 pandemic?"
I will point to this book. It is my lockdown work.
As the virus blew across the world like a bitter wind, I stayed in and did this. It helped to keep me sane.
In itself it is a small thing, but I want to dedicate it to the numerous people who did exceptional things in every country. Those who worked on the front lines and behind the scenes through it all to care for and keep safe countless strangers, friends, and neighbors.

I also want to thank my wonderful family for their spirit, sheer inventiveness, and support.

Also I must thank my amazing cocreators Genevieve and Alison who, lockdown or not, always have the best creative answers.

First US edition 2021
First published by Templar Books, an imprint of Bonnier Books UK, 2021
Library of Congress Catalog Card Number pending
ISBN 978-1-5362-1792-6
21 22 23 24 25 26 TLF 10 9 8 7 6 5 4 3 2 1
Printed in Dongguan, Guangdong, China
This book was typeset in Adobe Caslon and Bodoni 72.
The illustrations were created digitally.

TEMPLAR BOOKS
an imprint of Candlewick Press
99 Dover Street, Somerville, Massachusetts 02144
www.candlewick.com

Grahame Baker-Smith

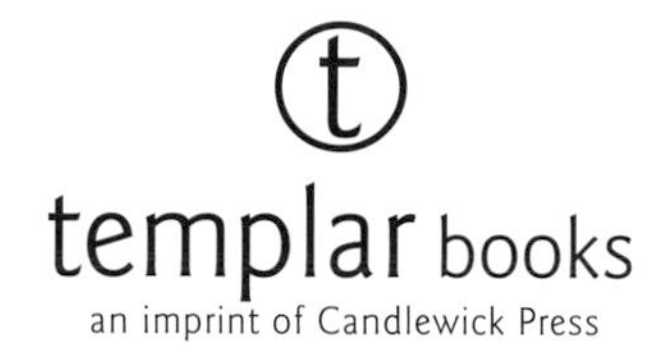

templar books
an imprint of Candlewick Press

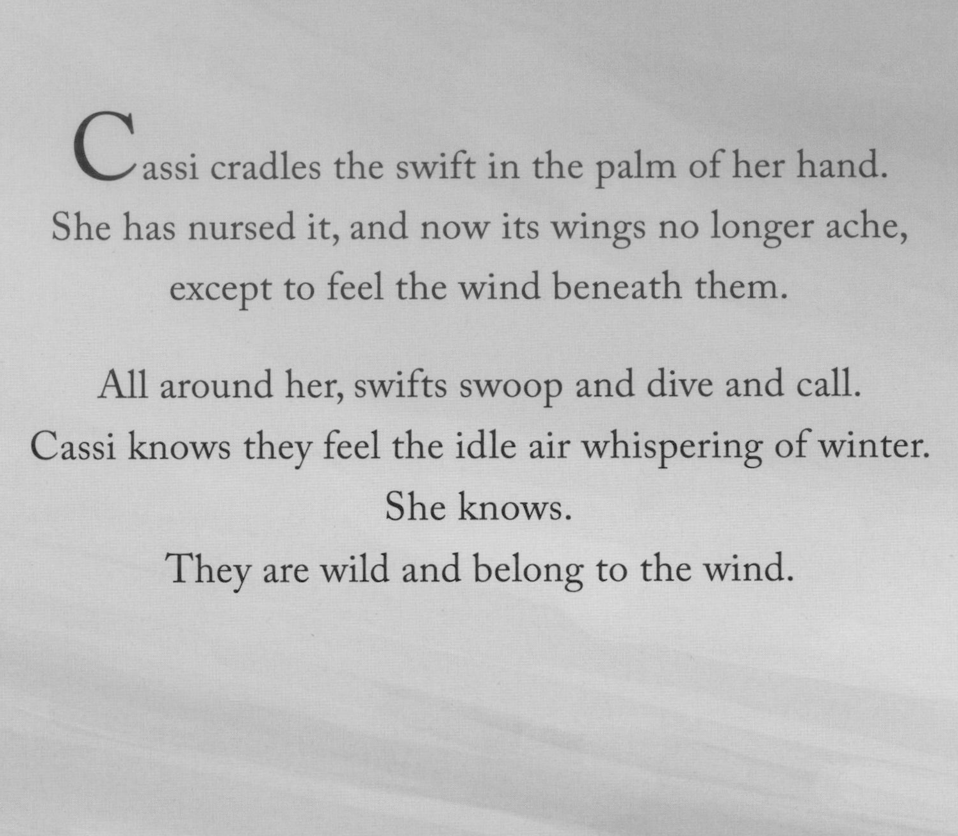

Cassi cradles the swift in the palm of her hand.
She has nursed it, and now its wings no longer ache,
except to feel the wind beneath them.

All around her, swifts swoop and dive and call.
Cassi knows they feel the idle air whispering of winter.
She knows.
They are wild and belong to the wind.

And so the swift waits,
sensing the stories in the air:
the fox in the thicket sniffing out
her supper, and small furry things—
scenting danger on the wind—running
for tree branch and burrow.

It feels the breeze that stirs the leaves,
urging the seeds of the butterfly trees
to try their nut-brown wings.
But the butterfly trees are not yet ready
to let them go.

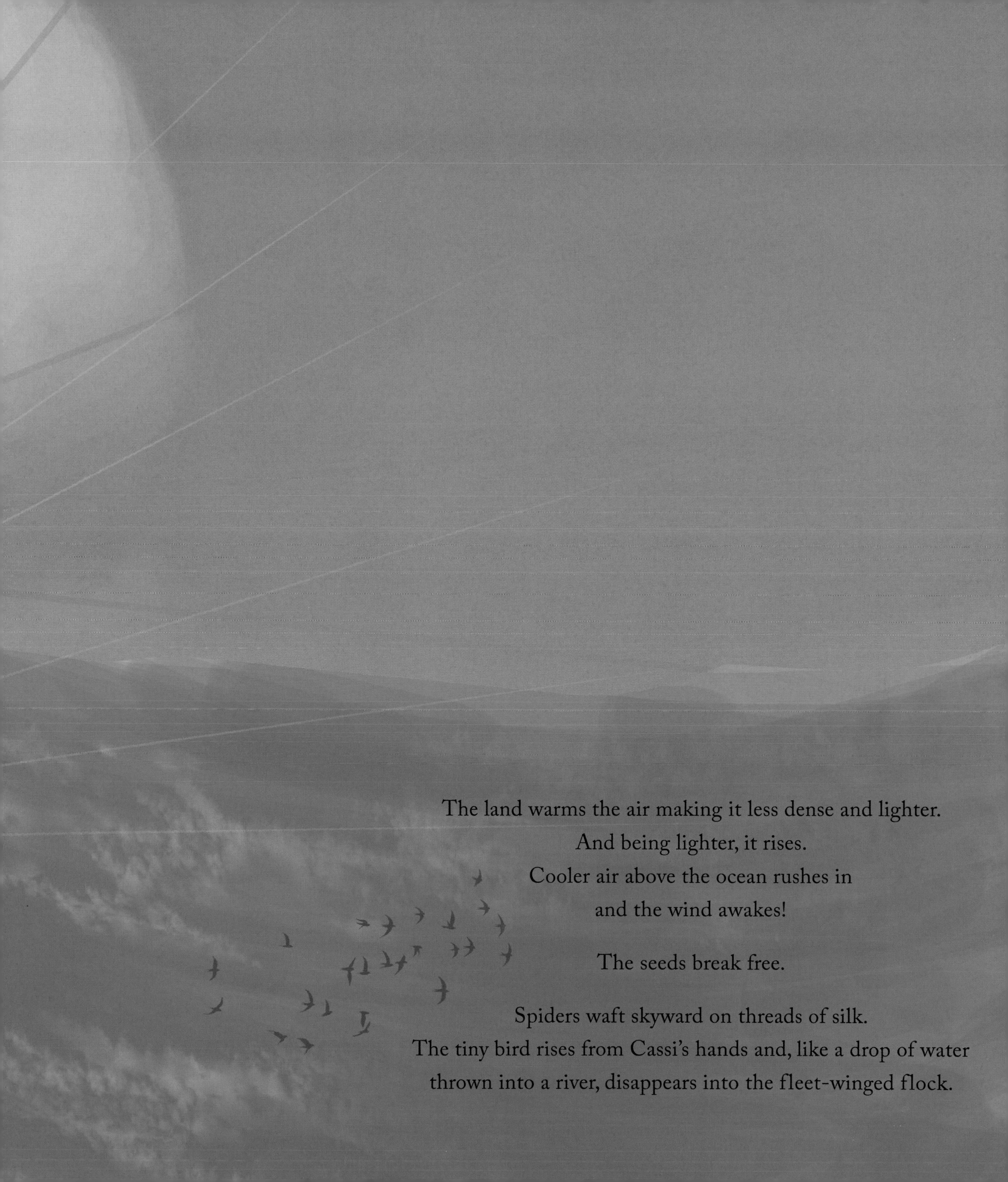

The land warms the air making it less dense and lighter.
And being lighter, it rises.
Cooler air above the ocean rushes in
and the wind awakes!

The seeds break free.

Spiders waft skyward on threads of silk.
The tiny bird rises from Cassi's hands and, like a drop of water
thrown into a river, disappears into the fleet-winged flock.

They know the path through the pathless sky.
They sense each twisting upward lift.
To them this is not new.
The wind is an ancient power.
Older even than they are.
And their kind go back to the time of the dinosaurs.

This pale revolving envelope of air, eggshell thin, is their home.
But it also turns our turbines to make our cities bright in the dark.
It has filled centuries of sails with the winds of trade and adventure!

The swifts have seen it all.
Around the still eye of a cyclone, mountains of clouds are carved
into a great spiral howling with stormy power.

The wind whips the waves,
cresting each one—like a conjuror's trick—
into wild white horses.

In the desert where a million years ago an ocean glittered,
the wind sculpts echoes in sand of those long-vanished waves.
For the wind is the ceaseless shaper of the earth.

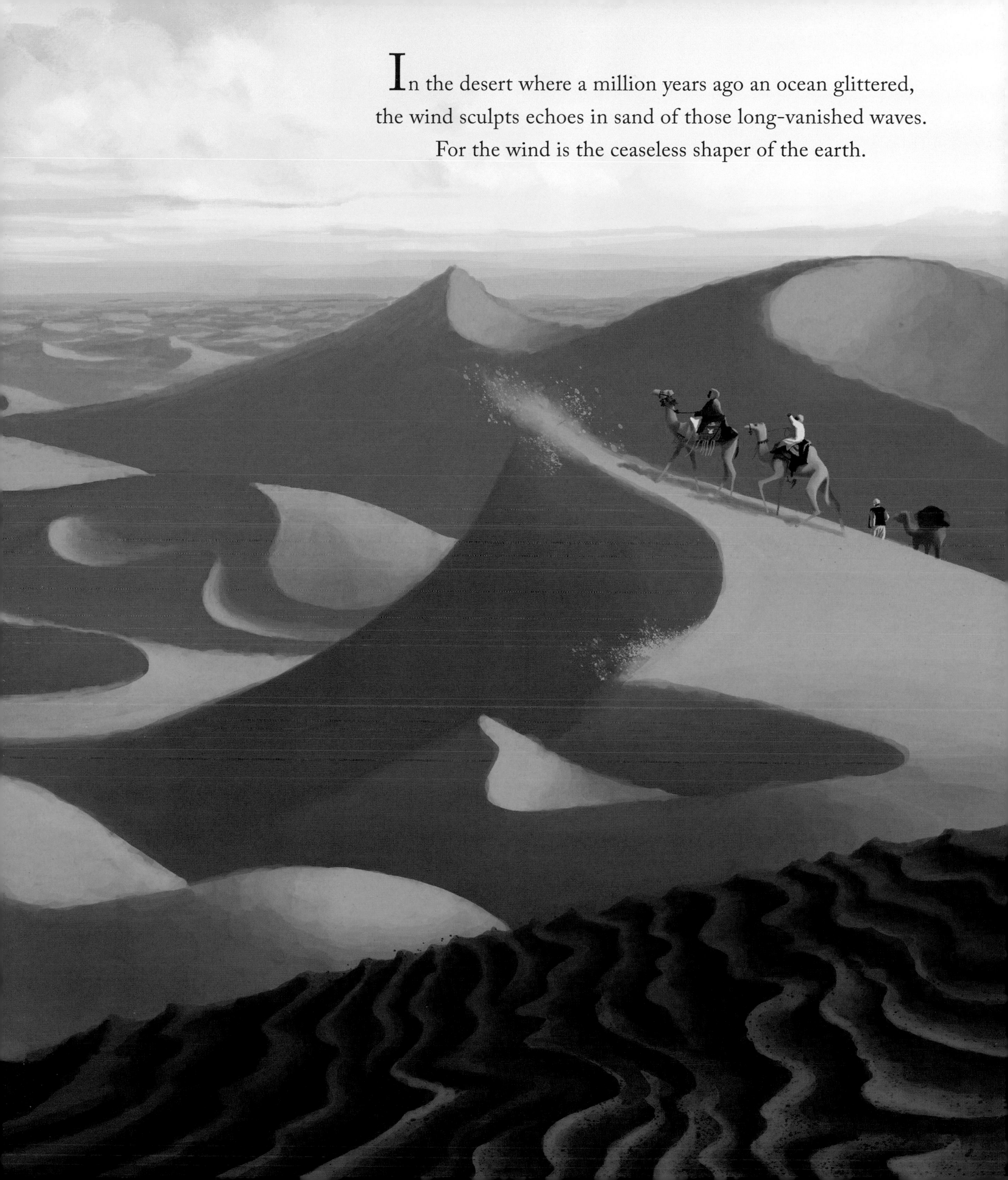

It will labor for a thousand years, grinding and blowing at bedrock
to make perfect streamlined shapes.
They poke from the ground like the fins of giant stone fish.

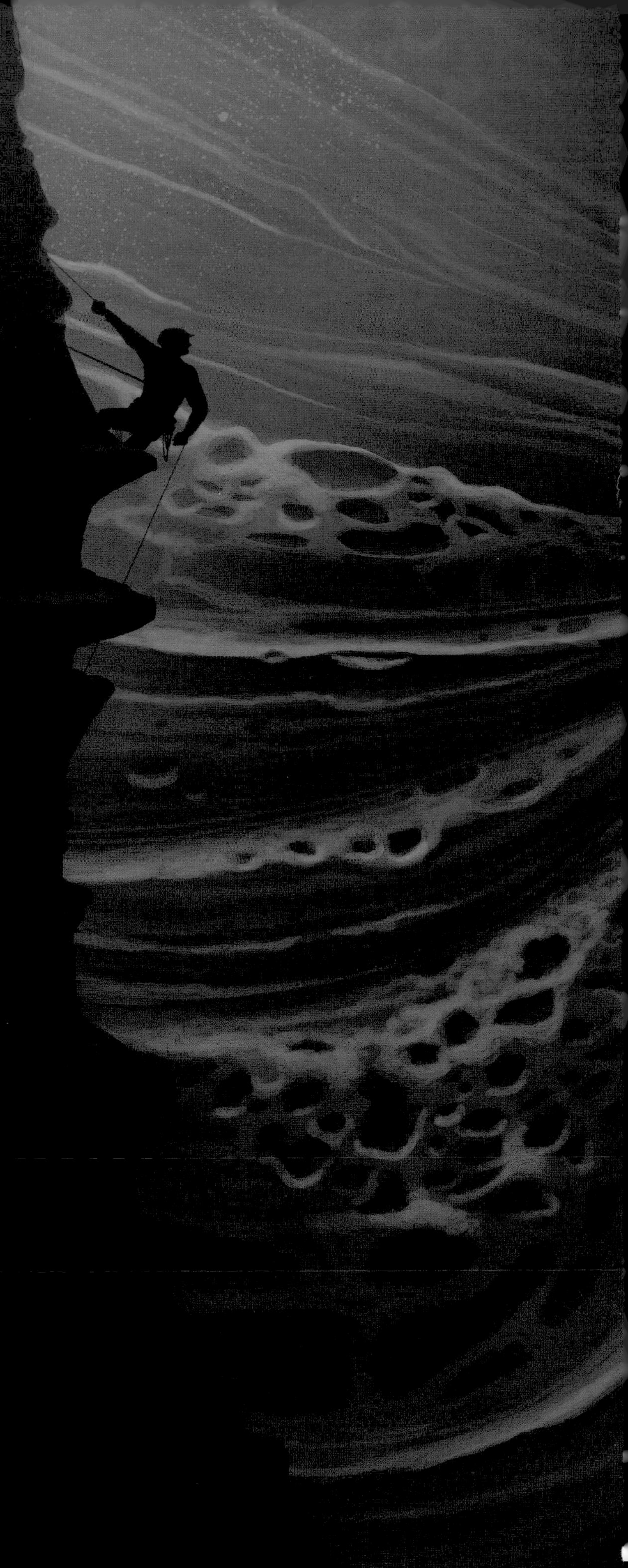

There are caves the wind has made,
like mouths in the rock.
Sometimes the air flows in, sometimes out,
as if the rock itself were breathing.

But sometimes the wind makes something on a grand scale.
For two million years it has carried desert dust
and particles ground by glaciers to make
a great plateau of rich yellow earth.

Above it the swifts
are near their journey's end.

Three months in flight.
Eight thousand miles.
Never once touching the earth to arrive at a place
far, far away from Cassi's healing hands.

A place where
Kûn has
been waiting
all the long
winter.

He jumps for joy.
He knows wherever the swifts are
summer follows.

Beneath the eaves, the tiny traveler
shakes the miles from its wings . . .

and rests

and waits for its young to hatch.

Briefly helpless . . .

they quickly grow fat

and strong.

They hear the call of the wild wind.

They already know the paths
through the pathless sky.

And when the time comes, they gather with the flock,
sensing the shift in the turning air.
They have promised the summer to elsewhere.
But they have deserts to cross . . .

and seas to span. And wild winds to ride . . .

and a summer to carry to Cassi.